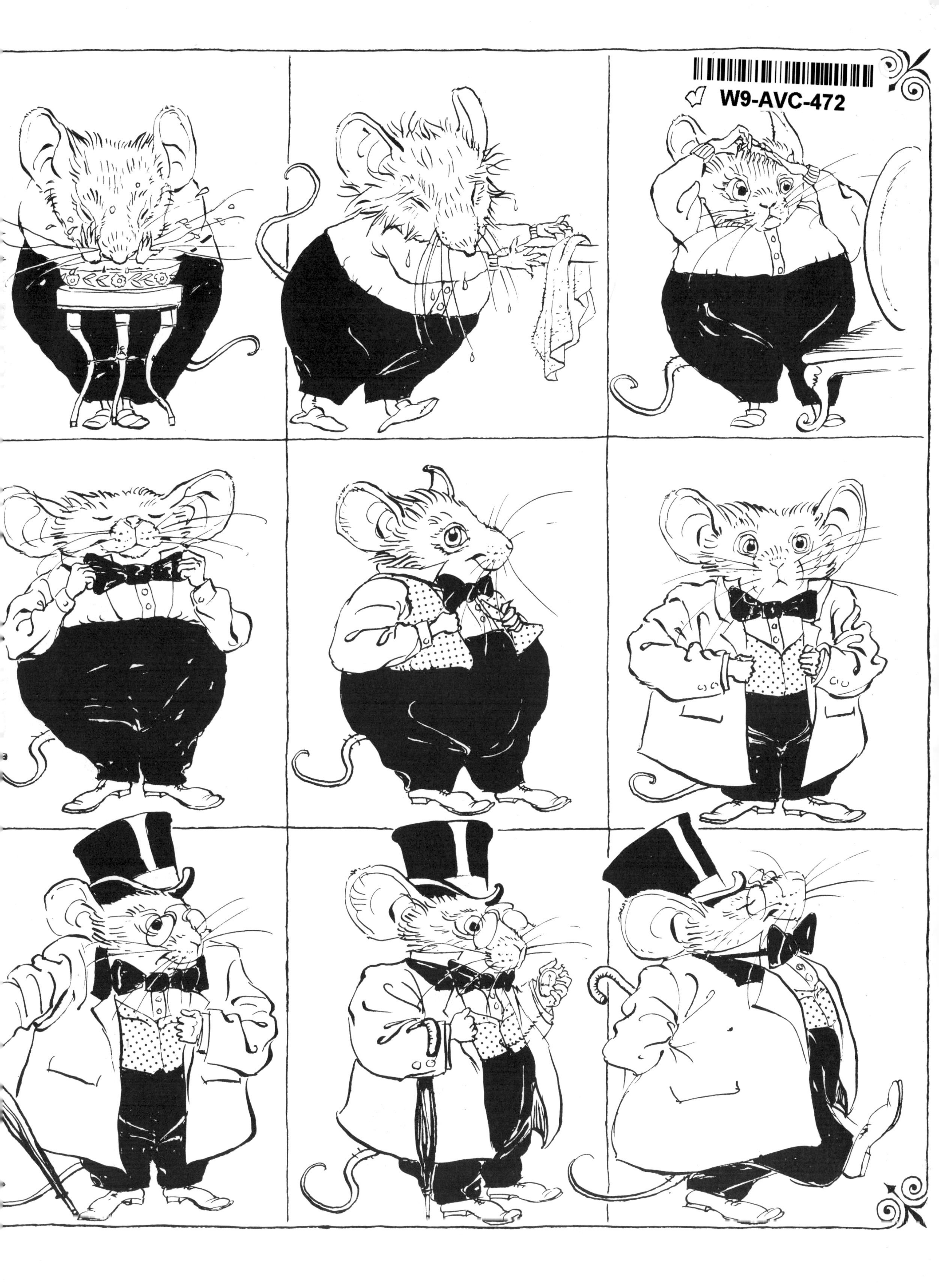

Happy Birthday!
Hailey -
Lots of love,
& Poppa
1998

THIS is the diary of a country mouse
Discovered in the attic of a dark, old house.
He wrote in his diary every day
And always found some things to say.

He traveled up, he traveled down
To city, country, village, town.
Saw many streets and many faces
And paused at many famous places.

His name was Mr. Albert Mouse,
Proud as Stilton of his spouse—
His wife, Victoria (like the Queen),
Was kind and pretty (never mean).
Their boy was Jack, their daughter Jill,
Like those who wandered up the hill.
So hear what Albert has to say
Of life in Queen Victoria's day.

DIARY OF A VICTORIAN MOUSE

Illustrated by

ANGEL DOMINGUEZ

Written by

LLOYD RICHARD

ARCADE PUBLISHING • NEW YORK

LITTLE, BROWN AND COMPANY

The Great Exhibition of 'Fifty-one
(Or was it perhaps 'Fifty-two?)
Drew thousands of gentlemen (ladies, too),
To feast their eyes on everything new.
(It was, I must tell you, a regular zoo!)

The flags of every country flew
From the roof of the palace of glass,
While gentlemen bowed and strolled on the grass
And elegant ladies said, "How do you do?"
(It was, as I said, an incredible zoo!)

Village Wedding

Wedding bells are ringing for Miss Celestine Mouse
And her proud and happy bridegroom, Mr. Nicholas Mouse,
In the charming little village of Titmouse-on-Grouse.
Let the bells ring out, let the neighbors all shout.
Before the day is over, before the setting sun,
Celestine and Nicholas will finally be one!

Boat Race

Oxford and Cambridge are rowing a race,
Rowing a race, rowing a race.
Oxford and Cambridge are rowing a race,
To see who's the better, to see who's the best.

The coxswains are counting, the spectators shouting.
They're surging and urging their favorites on.
Now Oxford is cruising and Cambridge is losing—
But wait! Oxford's losing and Cambridge *is cruising!*

Stroke boys, stroke again,
Till you've lost or you've won.
Go, Toad, and go, Badger! Go, Mouse, above all!
No matter who wins, everyone will stand tall!

House of Commons

The House of Commons is a place
To make a very serious face,
To sit with glasses on your nose
And listen while the hot air blows.

Now, Owl's been talking for hours, you see,
About the pros and cons of cheese:
"Should cheese be given to one and all?
To tall and short, to big and small?
Or only to the happy few,
To us, or them (and maybe you)?"

"Cheese! Cheese for all!" (A mouse's voice.)
"I said we need cheese,
If I may say so, if you please!"
So all agreed: it was the House's choice.

William Mousepeare was a poet
(Just in case you didn't know it),
The greatest in the world, some say,
And this the house where he did stay
With his dear wife Anne Hathaway.

Will's bringing wood home for the fire,
And flowers for Hathaway to admire.
But look at Junior Mousepeare's face!
Something's amiss, quite out of place!
He's cut a piece of Mother's cake,
Which surely isn't his to take.

Train

The train is clearly here to stay,
To span the land from side to side,
Crisscross the nation countrywide.
It's surely here to stay.

The horse is doomed. Long live the horse!
(We really hate to see it go.)
But trains go farther faster, so
Retire the horse with no remorse.
Come! Hop aboard, full steam ahead.
Long live the train, the horse is dead!

Loch Ness

In Scotland lies a lake called Ness,
Whose bottom is, I must confess,
The home of Nessie, bless her name.
She's prehistoric, some folk claim.

Local people swear she's there.
But when you ask them, "Show us where,"
They simply sit, or stand, and stare,
Then point into the morning air.

She's been there years and years they say,
Thousands at least and maybe more.
If you're patient, if you stay,
You'll one day see her from the shore.

Tourists come from far and near
To catch the slightest glimpse of her.
Toad claims he's seen her, Badger, too.
Hare thinks they're fibbing—now, don't you?

Scottish Dancing

Hear the high-pitched bagpipes play
Their merry tune this autumn day.
Clap your hands and tap your feet
To the rhythm of the beat.
Heel and toe, then toe and heel,
All will dance the Scottish reel.

Badger with his shepherd's crook
Stops — he wants to take a look.
Mole and rat, each in a kilt,
Hop nimbly to the music's lilt,
While toad, as smoothly as an eel,
On tiptoe trips the Scottish reel.

"Ah, this is the life," said Toad to Mole.
"This is the life for me.
The sporting life, the boating life,
The life of the lake and the sea."

"That's all very well and good, Mr. Toad,"
Said Mole with a gleam in his eye.
"You read your book while I tote the load,
That's not my idea of fair."

"Now, Mole, keep cool," Mr. Toad replied.
"Let's share and share alike:
You tote, I'll eat; you row, I'll read,
While we float in Windermere Lake."

The Peeler

(Pickpocket)

A wealthy mole was out one day
A-walking down the busy street,
His hat on top, his glasses perched,
And shoes upon his tiny feet.

When all at once two ferrets came
And whisked away his watch and chain,
And, as they say, with little pain,
His wallet, too, they snatched.

While Bulldog Bobby saw it not
(He was too busy with his thoughts),
Two other strollers saw and watched
The thieving ferrets stalk their prey.

They grabbed the ferrets by the ears
And shouted "Help!" so loud and clear
That even Bobby woke to see
And took them into custody.

Windsor Castle

Ring a ring of roses,
A pocket full of posies.
Hush! Hush! Hush! Hush!
We all fall down.

Ring a ring of roses,
Funny animal noses.
Atishoo, Atishoo,
The Queen has lost her crown!

Hatchards

Badger's bought a book, look!
Badger's bought a book.
Badger's bought a big, fat tome.
Badger's bought a book, look!
Badger's bought a book.
Badger's on his way back home.

Royal Academy of Arts

The walls are filled to the tippy-top
(It looks as though they didn't know where to stop!)
With landscapes and seascapes and portraits, too,
With something for everyone (including you!).

The crowd is all dressed to the hilt, to the nines
(In fact to the tens and, for some, the elevens).
They've come both to look and be looked at, that's fine,
And most of them think they have landed in heaven!

Punting

Punting is like rowing only more so.
It takes a very special movement of your
torso.
You let the pole down
Till it touches the ground
At the bottom of the river
Or the bottom of the stream.
Then you push off once
And you push off twice.
(It's not as easy as it seems,
Especially for us mice!)
Punting is like rowing only more so.
It takes a very special movement of your
torso.

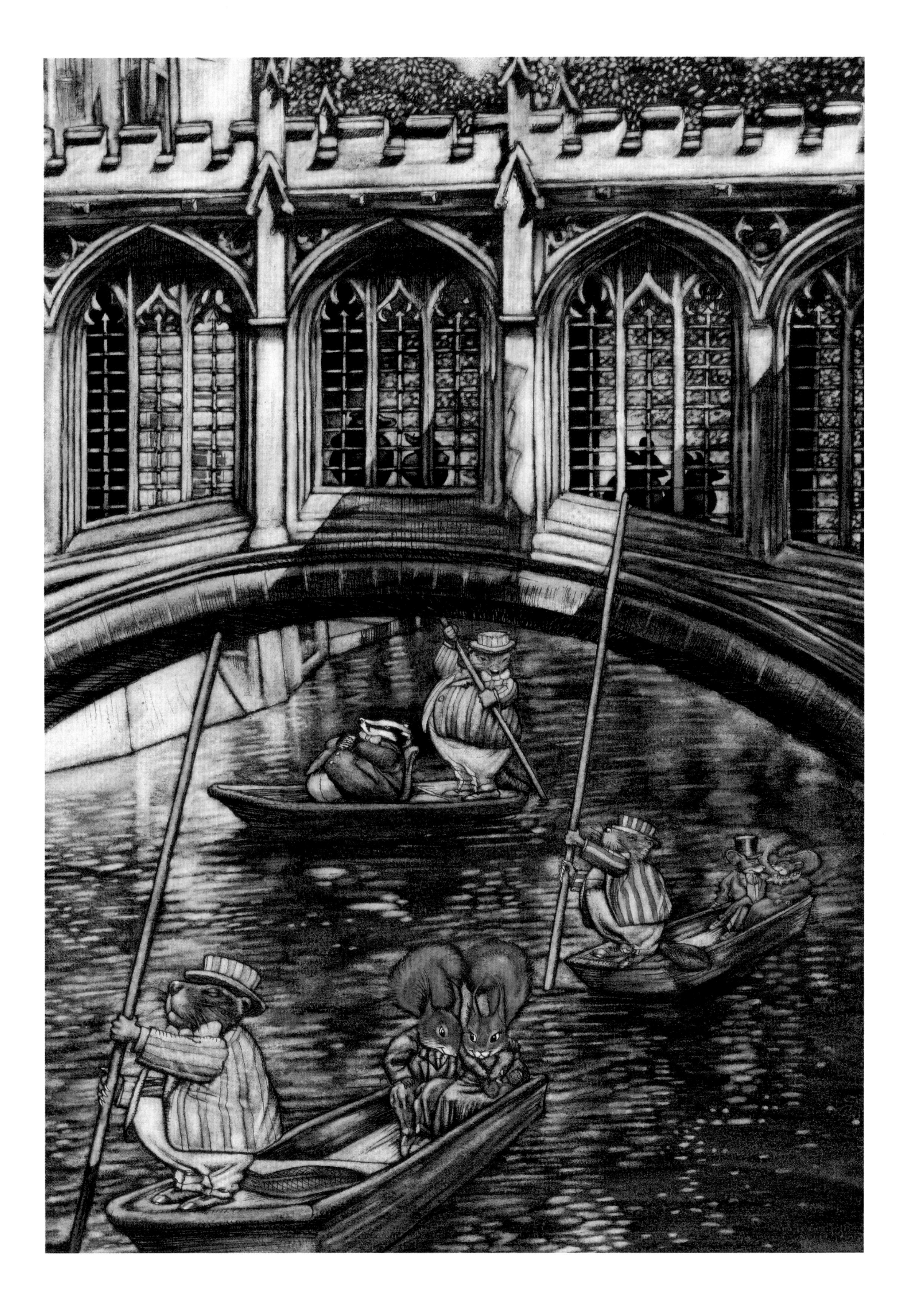

Irish Party

The Irish love to party, the Irish love to play,
The Irish love to sing and dance, almost every day.
They play the flute, they sip their tea,
They picnic underneath the tree.

They play the harp, then dance the jig.
(On music they are very big!)
They play the harp and dance some more,
Then clank their glasses and shout, "Begorra!"

Porcupine Pub

The Porcupine Pub is a prickly place,
So beware if you're there, if you show your face,
For when Porcupine comes you'd better look out
Or you'll have a prickle right smack in your snout.

Mr. Beaver, Mr. Badger, Mr. Turtle, Mr. Hare,
Always be careful when Porky's there.
He's a nice enough fellow, but when he turns
His prickles turn, too, and do they burn!

The Brighton Run

With a wobble and a rattle
And a rumble and a hum,
Off go the autos on the Brighton run,
Off go the autos on the Brighton run.

With a toot of the horns
And a cheer from the crowd
("Look out, they're coming," the policeman warns),
Off go the autos, all in a row.
With a wobble and a rattle, off they go!

Beach

Down at the beach two mice have made
Sandcastle mountains with their spades,
While out at sea the sailors race
Their sailboats at a mouselike pace.

Toad puffs up his chest and loudly calls,
"Let's play ball, folks, let's play ball!"
But no one wants to, what a shame!
Goodness, thinks Toad, we'd have had a good game!

Then a hoop falls smack onto Mole's long nose
(Mrs. Mole doesn't notice; she's having a doze),
But everyone there is pleased to be
Down by the seaside, down by the sea.

Professors meet at ancient places
(See how serious are their faces)
To argue why and where they came from:
"Who put these piles here anyway?"
"What mouse could carry them all alone?"
"Look at that big, that heavy stone!"
"It must have come from far away."
(Sometimes professors are very dumb!)

Christie's

Christie's is an auction house
Owned by Mr. Christie Mouse
(Cousin of Mr. Albert Mouse),
Where people come to buy and sell
Prints and pictures and bric-a-brac
(Some of which they then sell back)
To the bang of a hammer and the sound of a bell.

English Heritage's
Stonehenge
Avebury
Old Sarum
Prehistoric Wiltshire
Mysterious Stonehenge

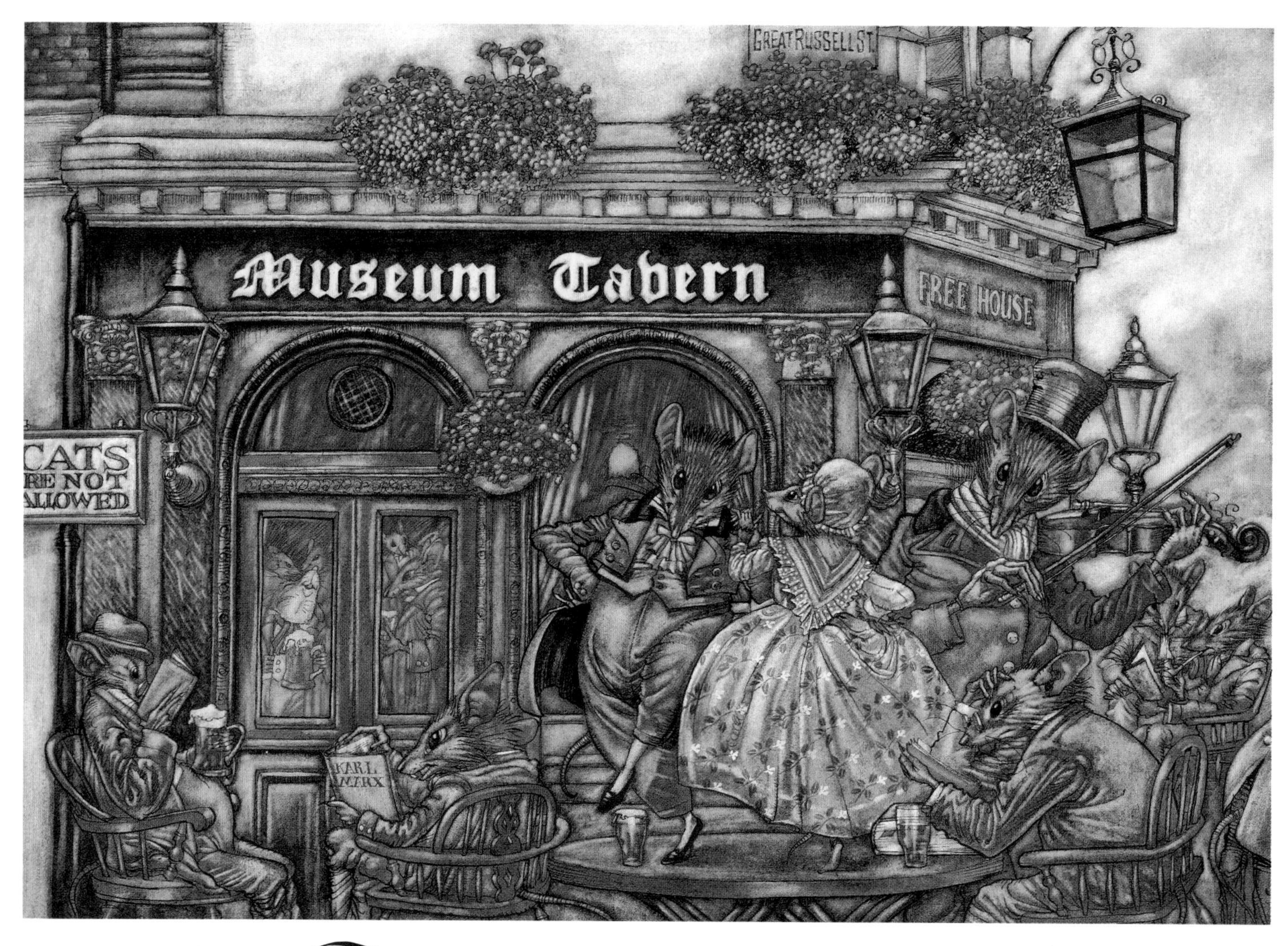

Museum Tavern

There is a tavern in the town
Where arms go up and drinks go down,
Where Father Fiddler never stops,
And people dance on tabletops.

Where some mice sit and read a book
While others sit and sip and look.
The tavern is a merry place
(Just look at Dancing Mouse's face!).

Another virtue of the place:
No Cats Allowed, which makes it nice
For all the shy and timid mice,
Who else might have to hide their face.

Reading Room

The reading room's for reading, you see.
It's a place to be very quiet,
Where you read and you look
At your favorite book.
You really ought to try it.

One day Mr. Toad, not knowing this rule,
Came in and sat down on the highest stool
And began to read and to read out loud!
"Shhh!" everyone whispered. "That's not allowed."

"Here silence is golden, isn't that clear?
If you can't be quiet you shouldn't be here."
Mr. Toad kept reading. All rose in a huff:
"Mr. Toad!" they all *shouted. "Enough is enough!"*

I fell asleep upon a hill
And dreamed of cheeses gold and blue,
Soft, creamy cheeses, hard ones, too,
The kind that mice love (don't you, too?).

And in my dreams I saw a crow,
Dressed in a vest, swoop down so low
He almost touched my whiskers, so
I stirred awake, then fell back still.

Just then a piece of cheese did drop
Into my waiting, watering mouth.
The crow flew off and headed south.
Was it a dream? Don't let it stop!

First U.S. Edition 1991

Text adapted from the work by Michael Cole

ISBN 1-55970-121-8
Library of Congress Catalog Card Number 90-62194

Library of Congress Cataloging-in-Publication information is available.

Published in the United States by Arcade Publishing, Inc., New York, a Little, Brown company, by arrangement with Michael O'Mara Books Limited, London

10 9 8 7 6 5 4 3 2 1

Designed by Simon Bell

PRINTED IN BELGIUM